I celebrated World Book Day 2015
with this gift from my local
Bookseller and Orion

Also by Marcus Sedgwick

And for younger readers

KILLING *the* DEAD

MARCUS SEDGWICK

Indigo

First published in Great Britain in 2015
by Indigo
a division of the Hachette Children's Group
and published by Hodder and Stoughton Limited
Orion House
5 Upper St Martin's Lane
London WC2H 9EA
An Hachette UK company

The Orion Publishing Group's policy is to use papers
that are natural, renewable and recyclable products
and made from wood grown in sustainable forests.
The logging and manufacturing processes are expected
to conform to the environmental regulations of the
country of origin.

A catalogue record for this book
is available from the British Library.

Printed and bound in Great Britain
by Clays Ltd, St Ives plc

ISBN 978 1 78062 239 2

For Steve, with apologies

We need to speak of the dead.

We need to speak *for* the dead, for they cannot speak for themselves. There are things they would want to say to us, if only they could talk. But, surely, they cannot. No longer can we walk into the next room, and find them standing there as they did in life, and hear what they have to say.

They are gone.

Yet . . .

Yet, they linger.

The most important person in this story is the one you will never meet. She is gone and yet she lingers, in the memories of those who knew her and lived with her. That is how the dead survive: they live in our memories, and some of the times that is a good thing and beautiful, and other times it is not good, and then the dead are like a virus in the blood, an infection of the mind.

Then, although we might wish to get rid of them forever, we cannot. We might even wish to kill them, but that is a mighty and nigh impossible thing, for killing the dead is very hard to do.

So it is with this girl who's gone now.

Her name, when they still said it aloud, was Isobel.

1

Beyond the lawn, the lure of the emptiness

Nathaniel Drake is the name of the new teacher. He walks through 1963 as if he owns it. He is young. He knows everything. He knows *everything*. Across the grass he comes from the residence he shares with Jack Lewis, the Head of English; the only two male teaching staff. The fine buildings of the school shimmer in young spring heat that is welcome after the winter; the Sarafian library, the gymnasium, the Halls, Main House, they sit and wait with unbreakable patience for Nathaniel to come across the lawn.

As he makes his way, he sees the grounds-keeper scowling at him, and remembers that Miss Grant asked everyone to stay off the lawn while it's made perfect for Procession Day. He thinks about moving onto the path but, taking another look at the groundskeeper, he doesn't.

Girls hurry along the red brick paths from the Halls to the school, the bell marking the start of the afternoon, but Nathaniel keeps his pace, because, as he says to himself, they cannot start without him.

It's a remarkable thing to look inside a mind like this. *He* is the newcomer, *he* is the interloper, *he* is the one who should be expected to feel out of place, yet he does not. Jack Lewis, who is also his boss, might be a middle-aged curmudgeon now, but on *his* first day at Foxgrove he cowered with the best of them. Foxgrove, the first and finest girls' school in the county, with its feet in an older century, in a time when things were done downright properly. Miss Grant, Head of School, is a doddery old thing, but she only needs to drop the words *the Board* into conversation for everyone to step back in line. This is a school among schools; two First Ladies, a noted actress who married royalty in Europe and three Olympians are among the girls who, like every girl who has ever been to Foxgrove, swept around the lawn on Procession Day in the Spiral Dance before sweeping out into the world that would give them everything they expected it to give.

It is a school that has beaten many into submission before Nathaniel Drake arrived here, and yet, he does not fear, he does not doubt. He knows he has the right to be here. He graduated from Cornell last summer, spent six months at his parents' summerhouse on Cape Cod, and though he has arrived late in the academic year, he knows he'll fit right in at Foxgrove. And if he doesn't, then they can fit in around him. His uncle is on the Board, after all.

When he arrives at his classroom to take a Senior English class, therefore, he expects nothing less than success. There are twelve of them in the room, twelve girls. Twelve rich girls, barely younger than he is.

He shuts the heavy oak door on the echoing corridor, and while his back is turned, allows himself a private smile at the hour ahead. What is the smile for? Does he really have no idea of what's coming? Was he so busy admiring the way he plans to teach this poem that he failed to pick up on any of the clues? And clues there are. Signals and hints, signs and upright facts that someone else might have noticed: the way no one uses the footpath that leaves the lawn and heads for the woods that separate the school from Stockbridge town, even though that would be the shortest way. Or the fact that along the wall of the proud hall, there are photographs of every Procession Day in the school's history, right back to a copy of a tintype made in 1863, the year the school opened, and yet last year's is missing. A more sensitive soul might have sensed an edge in the air in the staff room; or a nervousness even among the girls in the dining hall. Or the way that something empty in the woods, at the river, calls out with invisible beams of attraction; a missing something that would pull everything towards it, like the empty centre of a whirlpool.

But not Nathaniel Drake.

'Ladies,' he says. He gives them a half of a smile to let them know he can be fun, if they deserve it.

'Today we'll study a poem by a poet whose name should, I hope, be familiar to you.'

He pauses just the right amount of time to get the reaction he wants, before saying,

'James Sarafian.'

He's laughing at his own joke before he realises they are not laughing with him. Nothing.

Irritated, he turns his laugh into a stern stare, appraising the girls.

He has known them only a short while, these ladies who will in a few quick weeks be gone. There are the faces before him; America's best. They are young and rich and pretty and even the ones who aren't pretty have the money to make it appear that way. And there is always that one girl. Her name is Margot. He doesn't like it when she looks at him. He doesn't like it when she doesn't. If we were to crawl inside his blood we would find that his pulse lifts when he thinks about her. If we could hear his thoughts we would hear the words *those eyes* being said over and over.

O those eyes, he thinks. *Why does she look at me with those eyes?* And then his thoughts slip lower.

'Jennifer!' he says, taking his mind back to his precious poet. 'Surely you know who your library is named after?'

'Yes, Mr Drake,' says Jennifer, always the most eager of his Seniors, though even she seems reluctant to say more.

'Well?'

'James Sarafian was a former teacher of Foxgrove and also a minor poet. He died tragically in the last weeks of the Civil War in the early stages of the Battle of Morrisville.'

Jennifer as she always is; like a textbook speaking.

'Very good,' says Nathaniel, 'though I would disagree with your use of the word *minor*. *Neglected* would perhaps be better. I would argue that his poetry was ahead of its day, something I will ask you to explore this afternoon.'

In his mind, he remembers his six months at his parents' summerhouse. Lying on the day-bed on the veranda, watching the waves cresting in the bay, a yawning notebook open on the table beside him, an underused pencil tucked behind his ear. He knows he will write poetry one day, great and important poetry. It just didn't happen at the summerhouse. There was too much to do. Or maybe not enough.

He stirs himself, trying to get his lesson under way. Yet there is a flatness to the girls.

'We'll consider a poem that is very close to home. Open *American Poetry* at page 84, where you'll find the verses based around the school itself; "Stockbridge".'

Not one of them moves.

Not one.

'Did you not hear me?' asks Nathaniel, his equilibrium faltering. These girls are supposed to do what he says. It's that simple.

'Well?'

'Yes, sir.'

They mumble, and half-heartedly pull out their worn copies of the anthology that has seen better days, full of poems that have seen worse.

Nathaniel is not that stupid that he does not notice.

'Do you have some objection to studying this poem?'

He sees Margot looking at him with those eyes, those eyes.

'Margot?'

'No,' she says. 'Sir.'

He cannot read her expression. He is *that* stupid.

He hesitates, not knowing how to handle this, then takes a breath, puts his head down and for a second time tries to push out into Sarafian's most famous poem, the one that got him *anthologised*. Though maybe it wouldn't have been if he hadn't been blown to bits at Morrisville. That kind of thing lends an artist a certain ... what? Nathaniel searches for the right word in his head and then wonders how famous his own writing will be, especially if he dies some kind of romantic death soon after completing his masterpiece. He could go to

Vietnam . . . could have already been made to go, in fact, if it weren't for his mother's brother. Having a well-connected uncle sure does . . .

He glances at his class and sees that they are waiting for him to do something.

He straightens his tie and begins.

'"Stockbridge" is a complex poem. With just three hundred and fifty-four words, it makes multiple references to multiple themes; to be found here are religious motifs as well as pagan ones; it's a poem that takes us from the individual to the universal, and through time itself, with a brief pause on the lawn here at Foxgrove, as we become witness to the Procession Day dance which I believe you . . .'

He looks up.

Something is wrong.

The only face he can see that resembles what is happening in his own mind belongs to that Japanese girl, Tomiko, like him, a newcomer to the school.

He puts his head down.

'What I . . . what I ask you today is whether you can find mention of the war in the poem.

Can we even see a foreshadowing of his own death in the verses, or is that mere fancy? The civil war was halfway through when the school was founded. Sarafian was among the first intake of teachers at the school, but late in the war went to fight, and, as Jennifer said, was . . .'

He stops again.

A noise has disturbed him.

It is a girl, whose name he has forgotten for the moment, and she is crying. Her hand is over her mouth, trying to stifle the sound, but her shoulders jerk and tears trickle over her fingers.

He opens his mouth.

He wants to say the girl's name, but it will not come back to him.

There are only twelve of them.

The crying girl.

Jennifer, sitting right before his desk, squirming.

Tomiko, with confusion on her face now, though, he realises, that her puzzled gaze is directed at him.

And Margot, whose expression is still impenetrable to him. All he can see is her gender, and beyond that he cannot see.

In desperation to regain control, he says, 'Perhaps you should leave' and he means it to be only for the crying girl, but since he does not say her name, they all get up. All of them, as one, head for the door.

'No,' he says. ' I mean . . . '

But they are half-gone already.

Margot looks at him with those eyes as she passes.

'Perhaps we should leave,' she says, and again he cannot read the subtle inflection of her meaning.

The crying girl is pushing through the others to hasten away. Now he remembers her name, and as Tomiko passes by, the last to leave the room, he stops her.

'What's wrong with Becky?'

'They didn't tell you?'

He doesn't even shake his head, but Tomiko can see he has no idea.

'It's because of that girl.'

'Girl,' he echoes.

'It happened before I came. Last year.'

'Last year?'

'A girl died. That's why no one ever goes to the bridge.'

'The bridge . . . '

'The covered bridge. Jennifer told me that people drowned there. You know, in the old days. There was an accident. A girl died.'

'So?' Nathaniel says. 'So what? Why did . . . ?'

'The poem?' says Tomiko. 'The girl was the Procession Queen. Just like in the poem. Becky was her roommate.'

'Oh,' says Nathaniel, and he thinks, *Now I remember. Only I didn't really listen when my uncle was telling me that story, I was just thinking about getting the job*. Then he adds, 'That's terrible.'

Tomiko shrugs.

'I didn't know her,' she says, and walks off.

2

The lasting effect
of a single word

Margot Leya has been at Foxgrove for six years. She has seen teachers come and seen some of them go. She is more experienced than this new teacher and she knows it.

By the time Mr Drake has collected himself and emerged into the gloom of the corridor, looking for his Seniors, the girls are all gone.

All except Margot, who sits on the stairs to the second floor, nine steps up. She's leaning back on her elbows, on the tenth step, her palms turned down, fingers hanging loosely. Her legs are crossed and her left toe points at Nathaniel Drake, as he hesitates in the corridor. She wonders when he will sense her sitting there, and closes one eye, sighting him on the tip of her toe as if she is an assassin.

She tilts her head, then mouths, near-silent, the sound of a gunshot.

Drake stiffens, turns, squints up the stairwell.

It's bright outside and the window at the turn of the stair silhouettes Margot, making it hard to see, but he knows it's her.

Motes float in the sunlight that streams down from behind her like tiny worlds in the void of space. A moment hangs itself.

Drake opens his mouth, but finds he doesn't have anything to say.

By way of reply, Margot uncrosses her legs, and lowers one foot to the next step down, and stays that way. Despite the light into which he is looking, Nathaniel can see more than he should see, and he forces himself to look away.

Margot has the advantage – of height, of light, and of power – and, without knowing why she's doing it, she presses that advantage home.

'Isobel,' she says.

Drake frowns, and is determined to speak,

but finds that he is beaten, and scurries away, heading for the sunlight.

The word *interesting* passes through Margot's mind, and she sits on the steps for a few moments more, before slowly rising. She descends the staircase, wondering what to do with this small reprieve of time. English was the only lesson of the afternoon. She will not be missed for hours.

She walks into the sunshine, and finds the campus is almost deserted. It's hot and she dismisses the idea of finding her friends and hanging out; the thought of Isobel has put her in a strange mood. She rummages around in her bag, the new one that her mother gave her for Christmas, and finds what she's after: a packet of gum.

She pulls out two sticks, stuck together, and acknowledges them for a moment, holding them up to the sun between thumb and forefinger.

She nods at them and her eyes form a satisfied smile, then she pops both sticks into her mouth, and wanders down the side of the library, taking a small path that is the fastest way to get out of sight of Main House, chewing slowly as she goes.

Chewing the gum makes her think of the Village and that of course makes her think of New York and, therefore, home. Her parents come to her mind but she makes them leave again quickly, because she doesn't want what's coming to be spoiled; an afternoon of bliss, all for herself.

There are the woods ahead, and then she's torn. The woods make her think of Isobel and, before she can stop it, she remembers the day they went into town, just over a year ago.

Their assignment in Art had been to capture something of old Stockbridge. There were six of them taking Miss Ellery's class; Margot took Sarah and Evangeline with her, Becky and Jennifer stuck by Miss Ellery's heels, and Isobel, as usual, put herself as far away from anyone else as she could.

Margot tries to concentrate on today. On the afternoon before her, the here and the now. She chews her gum, heading towards the low hill where the trees give out at the top in a private theatre of the sky. She stares at her feet, stepping one after the other, to try and block her memories, but trying to stop it only makes them come stronger. She remembers how after an hour or two, with Miss Ellery and her willing pair holed up in the cemetery, she and Evangeline and Sarah got bored, put their pencils down, and wandered to the store to get a soda.

'Look,' Sarah had said, nudging Margot, and there was Isobel, sitting on the steps of someone's porch, across the street from the gas station.

Isobel hadn't seen them, but they saw what she was drawing; that boy, 'Man' Larsen's boy, who worked pumping gas and fixing fenders.

Wrapped into herself, by the time Isobel knew they were there it was too late; they'd seen a dozen quick sketches of the boy; some just his face, some his arms holding the gas pump, some full length as he disappeared into the workshop. The drawings were good.

Margot remembers the rest in snatches: ripping the sketchbook from Isobel's hands, the laughter, the teasing. The boy was sure a cutie. Sure. That only made them laugh the more. She doesn't remember that they even said anything to Isobel, they didn't need to. It was obvious what they were laughing about. Isobel, weird and plain, Larsen's boy across the street. Maybe she said, 'Cute'. She can't remember.

They tore Isobel's drawings into confetti that hadn't even finished flowering down to the ground by the time they sat down to order their drinks.

Now that she's done with dragging that memory back, Margot finally manages to free herself of it, and just in time. She needs to be in the right frame of mind; she's learned that's important.

She lies on the top of the hill, on the grass, with the trees around to protect her. The school is out of sight; her vision is only the sky and the gentle white clouds stuck to it. Perfect. She shuts her eyes for a moment, and when she opens them again, it's started.

The green tips of leaves twist the air into spirals.

Voices of ghosts come out of the air.

The ghosts of heaven.

She smiles.

3

Ink on paper

Jack Lewis has met some pups in his time, but this one beats them all. The new English teacher, Drake, sits across from him, on the other side of the desk. No, he doesn't sit; he lounges, as if this was *his* office, as if he was the old-timer handing out the lecture to the young snapper of whips, and not the other way around.

They are a cliché, the pair of them; it's just that only one of them is aware of that. Therefore, as Jack Lewis delivers the necessary admonishments to Drake, he cannot help but watch himself do it. He also watches the arrogant youth in front of him failing to react adequately to what he's being told, and he also reflects on what a terrible, miserable and utterly *boring* cliché it is to have to play the part of the disappointed senior teacher faced with the juvenile who knows nothing but thinks he knows it all.

Nevertheless, Jack Lewis also finds himself being rather good in his role and, being good at it, he starts to like it.

'What the hell were you thinking, Nathaniel?'

Lewis laces Drake's name with all the condescension he can.

Drake has the good grace to pretend to be apologetic.

'Really, Jack, I'm sorry. I –'

'Oh, come on, I'm not talking about the fact they walked out on you. Though that's bad enough. I'm talking about why the hell you were teaching that poem.'

'Well, you see, Jack, I didn't . . . I mean, I wasn't aware that there was a connection to the girl's death.'

Stop using my damn name, thinks Jack Lewis, *when I didn't give you permission to be*

*my equal. Stop using my name, and start using
'the girl's'.*

'Isobel,' he said. 'Her name was Isobel, and
I'm not talking about her either. I mean, what
the hell were you doing teaching that poem
when they've been taught it ten thousand times
already? Ever since they got to Foxgrove! Our
little school's one claim to fame; our poet who
got blown up. Jesus, man, couldn't you push
them a little harder? They're *Seniors*. They're
bored witless by Sarafian this and Sarafian that.'

Nathaniel blinks.

'Yes, Jack. I see that. I'll be certain to –'

Stop using my name, thinks Lewis. *Insolent
pup.*

'And do not let your accursed students
wander out of your classroom again.'

Lewis feels pretty satisfied with the level
of humiliation he manages to get into that
wander, and then decides he's bored with the
whole thing.

'Get lost. See you at dinner.'

Nathaniel blinks a couple more times, then
slowly stands up.

'I –'

'Dinner, Nathaniel. I will see you at dinner.'

Drake slopes off, still managing to make even the simple action of going offensive, leaving the door open behind him as he goes.

Lewis swears, loudly and satisfyingly, pulls his shoe off, and throws it at the door, managing to hit it so it swings closed sufficiently to restore his isolation.

Suddenly, his mind clears of his irritation with Drake, and into his head comes a name; *her* name: Isobel.

Isobel. Yes, these Seniors, who were his Junior English class last year, they were all bored with Sarafian. All but Isobel. She loved him, loved his poetry, and yes, he suspects she especially loved the fact that the young and gifted poet was killed on the battlefield, because that would have suited her kind of mind. She was not like the other girls, of that Lewis is certain. He doesn't remember when she first arrived at Foxgrove, because no one does. No one paid her any attention then; she's one of those girls your eyes just slide right past. There's always another student, another girl, who demands your attention, for one reason or another. The loud ones, the clever ones, the stroppy ones, the manipulative ones. So it was years before anyone noticed Isobel, and even then, she was only noticed *because* she was so unremarkable. If Jack Lewis thinks of her as she was then, as a Freshman, he struggles to bring her to mind. If he succeeds at all, he can see an awkward girl. Quiet, of course, introspective, but there was something more to her than that. No one paid her attention; she wasn't great at sports, but not bad enough to draw anyone's gaze either. Quietly, she did her classwork and quietly, she never excelled, but she never flunked anything. She sat near the back, but not right at the back, hiding at least one eye behind her straight black hair, hoping to get through school, through life, unnoticed.

But, eventually, people started to notice her. Jack Lewis was one of those people.

He found her on a bench in the Willis

Garden one afternoon reading Flannery O'Connor. That was enough to stop him in his tracks.

'Most people never get past Poe,' he'd said and, since she hadn't yet seen him, she shot back into the crook of the bench like a cornered mouse.

'You like it?' he'd asked.

She'd nodded. She actually spoke.

'But I don't like all the religion.'

Lewis had laughed happily at that.

'Nor me, my child,' he'd said, winking, and then, to his great surprise, he sat down and they chatted about writers for a good half hour; Poe, of course, and also Faulkner, and stranger fare, like Lovecraft.

Eventually, Lewis said, 'And what about the English?'

'The English?' she'd asked, her eyes widening.

So he'd talked to her, about Robert Louis Stevenson, and she pointed out that he was Scottish, and he talked to her about Yeats, and she'd pointed out that he was Irish, and he talked to her about Arthur Machen, and she pointed out that he was Welsh.

'So you know these writers?'

'Only by name. I haven't read them.'

'You should. If you like this stuff. This dark stuff. This mystical stuff. You do like it, it seems.'

She didn't say anything to that. She closed the book she'd been reading and, as she did, Lewis saw that the open page was drawn on, a finely wound spiral in the margin, in green ink. Only then did he see the pen in her hand, and the touch of green ink on her fingertips.

'Is that a school book?' he asked, annoyed at having to become a teacher again.

Timidly, Isobel had nodded.

Jack breathed out slowly.

'What's with the spiral?'

Isobel shrugged.

'Never mind,' Jack said, waving a hand at the book. 'No one else has ever borrowed it from the Sarafian anyway.'

He smiled. 'I'm going to bring you two books,' he said. 'I think you might like them.

Machen and Powys. And yes, Powys was Welsh too.'

He stood up.

'Sir?' asked Isobel.

'What's up?'

'Do you like Sarafian's work?'

Jack took a long look around as if he'd been caught stealing from the pantry.

'Love him. It took poetry almost fifty years to catch up with him. He was so far ahead of his time, no one could even see what he was doing back then. I think he was a genius. But don't tell anyone I said so.'

'Do you think he would have ever written a novel? If he'd lived?'

Lewis looked at the tiny wisp of girl before him, and couldn't work out why hearing such a perceptive question from such a nothing of a girl filled him with an almost unbearable mixture of joy and pain.

He almost winced.

'Who knows?' he said at last. 'It's a fascinating thought. In fact, some scholars have said that a page of free writing found in his notebooks indicated the seeds of a novel. Right, I'm leaving, but I'm going to lend you three books.'

'Thank you, sir.'

'Yes, thank you, sir,' he said, mimicking her. Then, relaxing inside, he added, 'actually, thank you, Isobel. You made my day.'

He made to leave.

'Sir?'

'What's up?'

'The seeds of Sarafian's novel. The page of notes. What was it about?'

Jack Lewis had his mouth open and was already telling her before he realised the small coincidence.

'Actually,' he said, 'they were rather strange. They were about, well, what you have added in your book there; the form of the spiral.'

'How can you write a novel about spirals?'

But Jack knew he'd spent far too long talking to this uncommonly well-read Freshman.

'I have a class to teach, Isobel. I'll bring you those books.'

So yes, Jack Lewis remembers Isobel now. And he can't help wondering how much of a part he had to play in her death. He tries, for the hundredth time in the past year, to put that thought away, somewhere so deep that it won't be able to surface again.

They were only books, he thinks. *I only gave her some books to read. They were only books, and books never hurt anyone, did they. Did they?*

Just ink on paper, that's all books are, just ink on paper.

4

From beneath the floorboards

Mei Ling never met Isobel.

Despite this apparent inadequacy, she shares a direct link to the dead girl, for she now sleeps in the bed that was once Isobel's. Juniors and Seniors at Foxgrove share the house known as Siegelton, named after Ms Ida Siegelton, who founded the school all the way back in 1863. The girls share large airy rooms, between two or three.

Mei Ling is another new girl, and has joined Foxgrove for her final year. Her father having moved from a post in Geneva to take a job in DC, she left her precious school in the Swiss Alps for the Massachusetts woodlands. But this is nothing new to Mei Ling; she has attended more schools than most teachers teach at in their entire careers.

Mei Ling has the bed that was Isobel's, between a radiator and one of the tall bright windows that lets light flood into the white room. Her roommate, Becky, was not exactly a close friend of Isobel's, because nobody was a close friend of Isobel's. But you cannot share a room with someone for three years without being affected by them in some way, even if that someone is as empty and quiet as Isobel Milewski was.

Mrs Grenjard, the Housemother of Siegelton, was perhaps as aware of that fact as anyone. You cannot raise (as she sees it) generation after generation of girls without learning something of the dynamics of their relationships, and she decided right from the start that it would be best if Isobel was only inflicted upon one other Foxgrove girl, not two. So she shared a room just with Becky Stewart for three years, and though Becky's friends were Jennifer and Mary and Helen, something of Isobel passed to Becky in all those long hours of homework, and through the long quiet nights as they slept in Siegelton House, the soft countryside breathing gently around the school as they did. That something had been enough for Becky to break down when the handsome new teacher began talking about that dumb poem in English class.

One evening, three days after the girls *wandered* out of Nathaniel Drake's class, Mei Ling discovers something. Becky discovers something too; which is that you cannot know everything about someone, even if you *do* spend three years sharing a room with them.

The room is white. White wallpaper, white curtains, white painted floorboards, though the paint is chipped and worn in many places. When the sun hits it, which is often because it faces south, it glows like a space of purity, and yet it holds something a little darker.

Mei Ling has Isobel's bed, and her desk. Of course, after she died, Isobel's things were cleared out and sent to her parents. All the many books that more than filled the allotted shelf above her bed vanished, to be replaced by a small cactus that Mei Ling has somehow managed to take round the world with her. The one picture that each girl is allowed to pin up was removed too, and all Isobel's clothes, so Mei Ling has a picture of a cat in a basket above her desk, where there was once a picture of a Native American earthwork known as Great Serpent Mound, and it's her clothes that now rest in what was once Isobel's chest of drawers.

On top of that chest of drawers, just in reach from the bed, sits a hairbrush, which Mei Ling now fumbles for.

She's clumsy at the best of times, and the hairbrush drops as she stretches for it, and then, with a curious bounce, disappears under the bed.

Across the room, Becky looks up from her book and rolls her eyes. Mei Ling is a quiet enough roommate but she does some really irritating things, and dropping almost everything she touches is one of them.

'Oh. Shit,' says Mei Ling, very carefully, since she is trying hard to be edgier like the

American girls, and is sure that swearing will help her case, even though she's not very good at it. Then she makes a great noise about rolling off her bed and scrabbling around underneath it for the hairbrush.

Becky looks up again, getting ready to roll her eyes, and instead has to stifle a giggle as Mei Ling's backside wiggles about, pointing up as she pushes in head first under the bed after the missing brush.

Then, as Mei Ling grabs the brush, and starts to back out, her fist leans on a floorboard which, unlike all the others in the room, moves under her weight.

She pauses.

She prods the floorboard again and finds that she is not mistaken; the board, which is a short one, is loose. She pushes her fingers and finds that by pressing down on one end, the far end lifts, and there is just enough light for her to see something beneath it.

'Hey,' she says, quietly, and then bangs her head trying to come back out.

She doesn't look at Becky as she stands and

starts to drag the bed away from the wall, and now Becky is rolling her eyes as if she's taking an exam in sarcasm the next day.

Mei Ling has the board in her grasp, and stands up with it, feeling really smart. She doesn't know what she's found but she's sure it's going to make her seem cooler to the other girls.

She stares at what's under the floorboard.

'What the shit?' she says, with exaggerated mannerism, to get Becky's attention.

Becky rolls her eyes some more, but she can't help but come over and see what Mei Ling has found.

'You don't say "what the shit", Mei Ling. That sounds dumb. You say "what the f –"'

She stops, stares into the hole under what was once Isobel's bed, and then she stares some more.

'What the shit,' she whispers, finally.

There, under the floorboards, exactly as Isobel left it on the day she died, is her secret library. Not the books that sat on the shelf above her bed, the obvious ones for schoolwork, and a few novels she read when she was a kid, but the books that mattered to her, the ones that fascinated her, the ones that obsessed her.

'What are they?' asks Mei Ling, but now Becky is way ahead of her, and starts to pull the books out into the light.

There are books on all manner of weird things, Becky can see that already. Some old books. Some notebooks, which are covered in Isobel's handwriting, and one really old book, from which pokes a single folded sheet of paper.

There's a knock on the door, and without waiting for a reply, Jennifer breezes in, wanting to nag Becky about the lacrosse match.

She stops straight away when she sees Becky on the floor with old books in her hands, a missing floorboard and Mei Ling staring at it all.

'I found it!' Mei Ling says, before there's any danger of any confusion, but Jennifer isn't listening. She's worked it out already, and then there are other girls stopping in the doorway and all staring and whispering and then there's Margot slipping into the room.

Hands go all over Isobel's library, pulling the books this way and that, and the room fills with noise as the girls start to ask what it means and as they read some of the strange lines in Isobel's own notebook and Becky tries to get all the books back.

Then Mrs Grenjard appears in the doorway and silences them all with a word. She's not a mean lady – she's caring and knows what living away from home can do to some of these girls – but she knows when she needs to be firm and hard and this is one of those times.

'What is this?' she says, but she too has already worked it out. 'These are not your possessions. They belong to Mr and Mrs Milewski now and must be returned. Girls! All of you in your own rooms and lights out in ten minutes. Becky, gather the books and bring them to my office please, right now.'

'I found them!' says Mei Ling, but no one is listening to her.

'Yes, Mrs Grenjard,' says Becky, and she begins to pile the books up.

'Margot,' says Mrs Grenjard, turning, 'I thought I asked all other girls to go to their rooms.'

Margot turns and goes without a word, but not before she sees what that oldest of the books was, the one with a sheet of paper poking from inside. It looked a hundred years old at least, and it was an edition, a first edition she guesses, of the only collection of poems that James Sarafian published in his lifetime: *Stockbridge, and Other Poems*.

5

First haunting

Mrs Eveline Grenjard has had some things to consider in her time as a Housemother; there have been thirty years of girls for her to bring through the school. What she has to consider now is the pile of books on her desk. A brief harsh word to the girls and calling lights-out half an hour before it was due was enough to get them in line. They are not bad girls, she thinks, and after what happened last year . . .

Poor Isobel. She cannot pretend that she cares as much for the girls as her own two children, now grown and gone. Yet at times it's hard not to feel something close to love for these bright, enthusiastic, innocent wonders to whom she plays surrogate mother. It's also sometimes hard not to be mad at them too. And then, what happened with Isobel . . .

She wonders whether she had any part to play in it. If what Isobel did to herself had anything to do with being named Procession Queen. When Miss Grant came to her in April, as she always does, to discuss who should be selected to lead the Spiral Dance on Procession Day, for some reason the first name that popped into Mrs Grenjard's head was Isobel's.

Miss Grant had had to struggle to remember who Isobel was, and then, after some prompting, had expressed surprise at Mrs Grenjard's suggestion.

Of course, the choice of a Junior was nothing that out of the ordinary; very often Seniors were selected, being about to leave for the wide world, but just as often a girl from the lower years would be given the honour of being Procession Queen. But what was unusual was that the girl was always someone of note; someone worthy, someone destined for great things and far-away places perhaps.

Isobel was none of these things, and Miss Grant had said so.

'Yes,' said Mrs Grenjard, now having to justify her choice when she didn't know why she'd made it in the first place. 'That's true, but maybe for once we should choose a girl who's not so . . . starry. One who represents the *normal* girl, who might not achieve great things but who should be celebrated anyway.'

Miss Grant had pursed her lips as she always did when thinking.

'Perhaps you're right, Eveline,' she'd said, 'but normal? Isobel?'

That nettled Mrs Grenjard for some reason and was enough to make her press her case.

'For once, let's celebrate the girl who's not going to go far, who's not going to marry a senator or represent her country at –'

'Very well,' said Miss Grant, laughing. 'You make a good point. Isobel it shall be.'

So Eveline Grenjard is thinking of Isobel as she hears a noise from down the hall. Sounds like one of the girls messing around. She waits.

There are times when it's easier to pretend not to have heard and let whatever's going on just simmer down.

Along the hall, in the room that Margot shares with Evangeline and Mary, something is stirring.

It's dark.

After being shooed away by Mrs G, Margot drifted down the hall, not even daring to answer her back, in case the Housemother saw that she had gum in her mouth. Chewing gum is forbidden on school grounds, a minor crime that seems to evoke ridiculously irate responses from the staff, which is one of the reasons that Margot continues to do it.

By the time the lights went out, Margot's roommates were already in bed, Evangeline cursing mildly at losing half an hour of their free time.

The girls went swiftly to sleep. The other girls.

Margot is drifting, however, but not asleep. A little light from the lanterns in the school grounds seeps through the curtains, picking out weird blue-hued patterns on the door, which faces Margot's bed.

She is staring at the shadows, fascinated by their form, when she sees them start to move. That doesn't worry her, not at first.

She sees that the shadows and the blue light are pulling at each other, playing with each other, like a dance. They move a little more, and start to twist and contort, and now Margot senses that something is wrong.

Her heart starts to beat harder, and her eyes fix open, still staring at the door, and now the door opens, and yet, at the same time, it stays shut. Despite remaining firmly closed, it unfurls like a flower and through the door comes a figure in a long white dress. Margot cannot see the face of the figure, but she does not need to.

The girl approaches through the unfurling shut door.

She comes closer.

About halfway across the room, she starts to float up from the floor, her white dress billowing around her, her black hair hanging down in clumps.

Margot is transfixed. She is unable to look away. She is staring at the white dress, the folds of which are forming shapes, figures and grotesque faces.

She tries to scream, but she cannot.

The girl in the white dress has paralysed her; her body is rigid and her eyes will not close, and now she floats up right over Margot's bed, coming closer, coming closer.

Margot feels a splash of something wet fall from the floating figure onto her face: a drop of water. Just a drop at first, but then another, and then another. She stares up at the girl above her, floating horizontally just inches from her own body, her own face, stiff with fear as now water starts to run freely. It pours from her hands and her dress and her hair and falls onto Margot, onto her body and her face, falling from the floating girl and into her open, gaping mouth.

Margot fights.

She wrestles against the paralysis, desperate to speak.

Finally, with enormous effort, she manages to gasp, 'You're all wet.'

The girl floating above her comes closer still, and now, finally, Margot can see her face.

She screams.

When Mrs Grenjard bursts into the room, she struggles to understand. She's seen girls have nightmares before, but this is different. Evangeline and Mary, who, to say the least, dislike each other, are sitting on Evangeline's bed together, clinging to each other as if their lives depended upon doing so. They are screaming and shouting, all at once, shouting at Margot, who is writhing in her sheets, her back arched off the mattress, the heels of her hands pummelling the bed, as she chokes and screams and screams and chokes.

'You're wet!' she screams. 'Why are you wet?'

She screams again and, attracted by the noise, the room is full of staring girls before Mrs Grenjard can manage to press Margot down and stop her thrashing about.

Evangeline and Mary are still holding each other, sobbing gently.

The staring girls are hideously quiet.

'Get out,' whispers Mrs Grenjard and, glad to be released, the girls flee back to the safety of their own rooms.

Margot has fallen into a deep and unconscious sleep, from which she will not wake for hours.

6

The Procession Queen

Miss Grant is a lady from another world. Another time. But that's why she is perfect as Foxgrove's Head of School. That's why she's been in charge for nearly half a century. Her predecessor, Ida Siegelton, who founded the school, was another such lady. A lady with a particular vision of how young women should be educated and how they should be made. Siegelton was a linear descendant of that same strong family who settled in Stockbridge, having moved from Plymouth and having bought a parcel of land from the Natives, to which they added over the years. Foxgrove stands on Siegelton land, land that runs away to the west until it reaches the Housatonic and to the north up to Stockbridge itself, taking in all the woodland in between, with Agawam River and the infamous covered bridge, site of a dozen drownings in a little over two centuries.

It was Ida Siegelton's interest in old English customs that had seen her recreate the Spiral Dance each May to celebrate the 'Procession' of her latest batch of girls out into the waiting world, an idea that Miss Grant thoroughly approves of, although she is utterly ignorant of its true, pagan origins. If she, or the parents, or the Board knew they were watching an ancient fertility dance every Procession Day, they might not be so pleased, because none of these girls should be having *anything* to do with fertility yet. Not for a long time, until they meet the right man with the right prospects and get married and have the right kind of children. Girls, preferably, who can come back to swell Foxgrove's future intake. Of course, over the years, there has been the occasional incident. The odd indiscretion, and once or twice even some consequences to be dealt with, to the shame of school and parents and girl alike.

It's time to choose the new Procession Queen, and Miss Grant knows it's an especially sensitive choice this year. After what happened with Isobel, and after they had no Procession Day at all, never mind a Queen, this year's choice must be just right.

She gets up from her desk and finds herself standing at the tall windows that look down across the lawn where the dance will happen. She is still ashamed that last year there was no dance for the first time in the school's history. There was no ninety-ninth dance, but that makes this, the centenary year, an even more special event. A chance to set things straight, to get them back on track, to make the traditions of Foxgrove come alive once more. To right some wrongs, for it was wrong what Isobel did. No one should take their own life; it is a sin against God, of course, but it was also a sin against herself, her friends, her school.

Why should she get to bow out – that's how

Miss Grant puts it to herself – *when the rest of us have struggled on without complaint?*

So Miss Grant is standing at the window, looking across the lawn watching the girls pass by on the red brick paths that link the school buildings, hoping to see the right candidate appear, as if summoned.

She's sure of one thing: she won't be taking Eveline Grenjard's advice this year, that's for certain. She railroaded her into last year's choice.

'And look how that turned out,' Miss Grant snaps at the empty room.

What she wants this year is a strong girl, one who'll relish the honour of being Queen, a fine-looking girl, someone sporty, for Excellence in Sport always sends out the right message to parents, and certainly not someone who'll bring the school into further disrepute, whether it be from suicide or *issues* of fertility.

It's more than ironic then, that at that very moment, into Miss Grant's field of vision strolls Margot Leya, and there and then, looking at her tall figure, her immaculate dress, her radiant hair and her refined walk, Miss Grant chooses the Procession Queen for the centenary dance. It's an open secret that Margot has always wanted to be made Queen; so why not give it to her? She won't buck and crumble; she'll make the very best of it, and do the school proud.

Just look at the way she holds her bag, Miss Grant thinks. That's a Foxgrove girl. And it's an expensive bag too, no doubt holding Margot's schoolwork, for which she will achieve high marks, and make us proud.

Yes, that's a Foxgrove girl, all right.

There's a knock at the door.

Mrs Grenjard enters, rather uncertainly, though this is something that Miss Grant does not notice, delighted as she is to have made her choice. But before she can inform the Housemother of this fact, Mrs Grenjard has something she needs to unburden herself of.

'You remember those books we found, that were found, the other evening?' she says. And before Miss Grant can do more than nod, Mrs Grenjard goes on. 'Isobel's books? I've had them in my room since then. I haven't touched them since. I mean, no one has touched them since. They have been sitting there since –'

Miss Grant decides to intervene.

'Eveline. What is the matter?'

'The books. No one has touched them. I've been trying to contact Isobel's parents but –'

'But what?'

Mrs Grenjard takes a deep breath.

'One of them has gone missing.'

'Are you sure?'

'I'm sure. I told you; I haven't touched them. No one has been in my room since . . . Yes, yes, I'm sure of it. Quite sure. One of them has been stolen.'

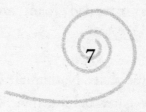

7

The Woods

Margot walks along the red brick path from the Sarafian towards Siegelton House, her bag bumping at her hip. It's been a couple of days since her disturbed night, a couple of days during which at first even the girls closest to her, Evangeline and Sarah, kept their distance ever so slightly. Now, she's glad to find that, as fast as the news went round the small school, the fuss seems to have blown over. Which is not to say that there wasn't some muttering in the showers one day after lacrosse.

Joan, almost as quick-tongued as Margot herself, came right out with it.

'So what happened to you?

'Nothing,' said Margot. 'Bad dream.'

'Bad what?' quipped Joan, and left it hanging.

Margot knows that Nathaniel Drake is walking a few paces behind her. She knows that he is looking at her. He, on the other hand, doesn't know if she knows. But if she *does*, then the fact that she's just made her walk a little bit more provocative can mean only one thing.

Eager not to seem too eager, he hangs back a touch, watching the flick of her skirt as she heads to a corner of the Siegelton building. Just before she disappears out of sight, she reaches a fingertip down and scratches an itch that has suddenly developed on her thigh about three inches above the hem of her skirt. He looks up and sees that she is looking back and has caught him looking. She smiles.

Drake stops for a second, and glances around. He scans a few windows nearby. Nothing. He doesn't notice that Miss Grant has just turned away from her window but, to be honest, Miss Grant hadn't even seen him.

Suddenly panicking in case she, Margot, goes, he hurries around the side of Siegelton House, and almost bumps into her.

From here, the sports fields spread away, sloping down gradually towards the trees that mark the edge of the woods. There is no way they can be seen from the main school house, or indeed from anywhere. They are alone.

'Mr Drake,' says Margot, her eyes pinning him to the spot.

'Margot,' he says. He can think of nothing else to say. There is nothing to say. He ought to walk on past her, maybe enquire if she's working on that assignment yet, and get on with his day. But he doesn't. He stands, looking at her, shifting his weight, suddenly, for the first time since he arrived at Foxgrove, feeling out of his depth, feeling as if he does not belong, as if he is no longer superior to everyone and everything.

Margot smiles at him.

He cannot think of anything to say, he can only think of what he wants to do. But she's saying something.

'Mr Drake,' she says, very slowly. 'Nathaniel. I have something you want.'

The words fall into the space between them.

He should let them lie there.

He should go.

He can deny everything and anything up to this point. He has said nothing. He has done nothing. He should turn and go and find a job in another school. In another state. Or maybe even Canada.

'You do?' he says.

'I do,' she says. 'Come with me to the woods. Won't you? And I'll give it to you.'

As they reach the first trees, everything changes. Crossing the threshold into the woods, Drake's fear leaves him. They cannot be seen from the school now; on the way out across the fields he kept checking back to see if anyone was watching. He could have told her to go on ahead, and he would follow behind, but he didn't think of that. He just wanted to get her to the trees as quickly as possible, and now that the green comfort of the trees enfolds them, he grows bolder. He lets his hand bump against hers as they walk along a leaf-strewn and overgrown path.

Other things change; Margot, for example. She has become a little less sure of herself, if anything. But she's come this far.

'This looks like a small road,' says Drake, meaning the path underfoot.

'It is. Or it was,' says Margot. 'You can get to town. It was the old way, but no one uses it now.'

Hardly anyone, she adds, to herself.

'Where are we going, Margot?' Drake asks, and now he lets his voice insinuate things, just as she did before.

'The woods.'

'We're in the woods. So what do you have?' he asks. 'That I want.'

It's been a fine day, but it's April, and from nowhere spring rain begins to fall. The canopy of the trees holds back the water only briefly before large drops start to fall on them.

Drake is squinting through the deepening gloom of the woods.

'Is that a house there? A barn or something?'

Margot doesn't need to look.

'It's a bridge.'

'Oh, right. The covered bridge. Why don't we go there before we're drenched?'

She wants to say no but he's already heading off down the path. She follows, speeding up after him as the rain starts to fall more heavily, and then she thinks three things to herself in quick succession.

I haven't been there since it happened.

Maybe I ought to go back.

Maybe it'll be fun to go back.

So she does.

He's there ahead of her, and is inspecting the old Massachusetts covered bridge like a genuine tourist.

'I never worked out why they built these things. The rest of the road isn't covered, is it? Why just the bridge?'

The bridge is like a long narrow barn, with open ends where the road runs through it, and sides open to latticework from just about chest height up. There's a spot where the roof has broken and rainwater falls in. Drake dodges the shower to peer through the latticework at the river below, which is a surprisingly wide, deep and fast thing to find in this otherwise peaceful woodland. There's an evil, dark brown pool directly under the bridge.

He remembers the stories of the drownings. Of *that girl*, and now he makes the connection that this must be where she drowned.

'Hey,' he says, 'Perhaps this isn't such –'

'They were built to protect the bridge itself,' Margot says, cutting him off. 'A covered bridge lasts about four times as long as one that's open to the elements.'

'Oh,' says Drake. 'Yeah, I guess that makes sense. How did you –'

'Mrs Fisher's Geography class.'

'Oh. Right.' He moves close to her. Very close to her. 'So, what have you got for me? Margot.'

Margot is annoyed. Her game is not working the way she wanted. She wants to just turn round and stomp back home, but something stops her. But it's all wrong now, the tension has gone. He's getting pretty sure of himself too, and she doesn't like that.

But she's here now.

She puts a finger out and hooks it behind his lapel, all the power it requires to make him move in towards her. She feels the wall of the bridge nestle into her back, and he presses in a little closer, looking down at her intently.

She reaches down, between the slight space that remains between their bodies, slides her hand into her bag, and pulls out a book, an old book.

'I thought you might want this.'

Drake takes a moment to realise that she's holding something for him to look at. He steps back, confused, and sees the book.

'What's this?' he says. He's annoyed, already sensing she's been playing games with him.

'I thought you might like it,' she says innocently. 'Sir.'

'What is it?'

'Look.'

He takes it from her, and some of his irritation leaves him as he realises he's holding a first edition of James Sarafian's *Stockbridge, and Other Poems*. It must be worth three thousand dollars, at least. He sees the folded sheet of paper tucked into the book, obviously something much newer.

'What's this?'

Margot shrugs.

'I don't know. Don't care,' she says, then sweetly adds, 'but I thought it might be something you'd like to have.'

Drake pulls the sheet of paper from the old pages, and sees that it's a Xerox copy of a double page spread of someone's notebook.

It doesn't take much of a leap to work out that he's looking at a page of notes by Sarafian himself, notes for something prose-based, not verse.

'You're right,' he says. 'I do want this. Where did you get it?'

Margot shrugs again, pins him with those eyes.

'Maybe you don't want to know.'

'Maybe you're right.'

'Good boy,' she says.

He moves in closer to her.

'So what do you get?'

'Pardon me, sir?'

'So what do you want for it?'

'Want, sir? I just wanted to make you happy.'

She tilts her head up to him, her lips bright with deep red lipstick, the smell of Wrigley's still on her breath, a combination that makes her mature and immature all at once.

'So make me happy,' Drake says, and puts his mouth on hers and a hand on her thigh.

There.

She got it.

'Mr Drake!' she exclaims, and pulls herself away. 'What are you doing?'

Drake turns on her angrily.

'Now just wait a minute –'

'I just wanted to give you the book. And, anyway, I have a boyfriend.'

She tries to pretend to cry and pushes away from him, back out into the rain, running for the school. And no, she wouldn't call Jimmy Harkness her boyfriend, but they've done it enough times, right there, under the covered bridge, so what's the difference?

Nathaniel Drake stands and watches her go, his heart pounding with rage and his fingers tight around Sarafian's book.

'What just happened?' he says aloud. 'What just damn well happened?'

He stands that way for twenty minutes, playing out what to do in his mind. He can deny everything. He didn't do anything. She led him on. No, don't admit to anything. She's just a fantasising schoolgirl. Wouldn't be the first time. There's nothing to prove to anyone.

He sighs, calming down. Best thing is just to wait. Give it half an hour, then take a stroll back to the school. If anyone's missed him, he can say he got caught out in the rain. It's already starting to ease now. There. That's the thing to do.

At the weekend he can drive himself down the Mass Pike to Boston and get the book valued.

Must be three grand at least. Maybe three and a half.

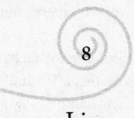

8

Lies

Jack Lewis, for some reason, is the last to find out that Isobel Milewski's secret library has been found. He comes to Eveline Grenjard's rooms one evening after dinner.

The two don't have much to do with each other; they have both been at the school a long time, but occupy different worlds, which rarely intersect. As she waves him into a chair by the unlit fireplace, he reflects that this is the first time he has been in her rooms.

'Yes, some books were found,' she says, pouring him coffee.

'Ah, they were? That's what I heard. Yes,' he says. Then, when she says nothing, 'Would it be possible to see them?'

'See them? Yes. Is there some reason you . . . ?'

'Yes,' he says, as matter-of-factly as he can. He's thought about this a lot and though he doesn't really want to admit to lending his own books to a Junior, in case it were misconstrued, he can see no other way.

'Yes,' he says, as Mrs Grenjard goes to fetch the stack of books, 'Yes, Eveline, in fact I loaned Isobel a couple of books a few months before she . . . A few months before. I just wondered if they were among those that were found. A couple of books. It may have been three, actually.'

But as she returns with the pile, he can immediately see that the Sarafian first edition is missing.

'This is all of them?' he's asking, but he's wondering why he trusted a Junior girl to look after a book that had cost him five hundred dollars to buy, twenty years ago. He's wondering that, but he knows why. He felt as though he sensed something in the girl; something bigger and better trying to get out of someone handicapped by their shyness and their awkwardness and their alone-ness. In some blunt way he thought that trusting her with a valuable book might show her that he respected her, and that that alone might be enough to bring something out of her. He'd let her know very clearly that the book was valuable, and as she'd nodded, and told him she'd be careful with it, he knew he'd made the right decision. He wonders if she'd made this library of hers under the floor then, or whether it was already waiting for its most prized item to arrive.

He pulls out the Machen and the Powys from the pile, indicates his name on the flyleaves to Mrs Grenjard.

'These were two of them, but there . . . You're sure this is all of them?'

He cannot bring himself to admit that he loaned Isobel the Sarafian. He looks Eveline Grenjard in the eye.

'This is all of them?'

She holds his gaze and, as flatly as she can, says, 'Yes, Jack. Quite sure. Why?'

'No, I . . . Well, there might have been a third. I can't quite . . . No, I guess it was just the two books. Just a couple.'

He can't bring himself to give in quite like this, but he doesn't have any option. Still, he's reluctant to go. Trying to find a reason to stay, he pulls out a couple of notebooks from the pile.

'What are these? Isobel's?'

'Oh, yes, but I don't think we should –'

'Why not? She's gone. What harm can it do now? She was a bright girl, that one.'

Eveline Grenjard leans over.

'You thought so too?'

'Yes, but well hidden, right? She was one of those girls who you just want to –'

'– to be able to set straight,' Eveline finishes for him. 'To help.'

'Exactly. Just get them on the right road.'

There's a moment of stillness as they realise they have more in common than either of them knew, and then Jack's leafing through the notebooks.

There's Isobel's green ink. Just its colour is

enough to bring him close to tears. He knows what the green means. It was a way, a pathetic way, of trying to be a little different, of saying, 'Here I am, and I'm me,' a way to try and break out of the prison of her own confinement. Jack knows it for a fact, because he did exactly the same thing when he was fourteen.

He focuses on her words, and realises he's reading a scene from a book. But it's a scene from a book that was never written; it was never written by James Sarafian, and now it will never be written by Isobel Milewski, either. But she's taken that page of notes, those seeds of Sarafian's, and developed them into a scene. It's set in the past, though it's hard to be sure when.

He finds that he is standing in a workshop of some kind. Carpentry tools are spread on the bench beside him, curls of wood shavings lie in little spiral forms all about him, on the bench, on the floor. He hears the scrape of a spoke shave and turns to see a man working on a long wooden box. The man is middle-aged, heavy, and his hands are both powerful and delicate at the same time. He lifts his head and sees his visitor.

'You know they used to use nails,' he says. 'In the old days. Poor folk still do. Not the best idea, a nail in a coffin.'

The visitor says nothing, but in his mind, he asks, Coffin?

The man nods, smiling. He picks something up, and shows it for inspection. It is a long brass screw.

'That's better,' he says. 'Better than a nail. Notice anything about it?'

The visitor shakes his head.

'The screw runs widdershins. Back to front. 'Gainst the clock. All other screws in the world turn the other way to this one. But coffin screws are different.'

A word forms in his mind.

Why?

The coffin-maker smiles.

'To stop them coming back, of course.'

The visitor closes his mind for a moment and, with it, his eyes.

The dead never come back, do they?

*

Jack turns the page, but there is no more.

No more writing. What there is instead, are spirals. Dozens of them, hundreds of them, in green ink, drawn on page, after page, after page, filling the remainder of the notebook, thousands and thousands of interlocking spirals.

He hands the pages to Eveline.

It's hard to speak without tears trying to choke him.

'Did you . . . did you see this?' he manages, and Eveline nods, sadly, both of them aware of the spirals' message.

Yes, perhaps just the obsessional interest of a teenager. They both know the way young people get, sometimes. Or maybe it's something more. Something darker; a hint of the madness that must have played a part in Isobel taking her own life.

Jack can stand it no more, and for the first time in over forty years, as Eveline puts an arm across his hunched shoulders, he weeps openly.

9

Second haunting

Margot, when she hears that she is to be Procession Queen, is overjoyed. She even phones her mother to tell her the news. For a moment there is a connection between them, as there used to be when Margot was still a little girl, and when her mother still cared about her. But then Margot can tell that her mother is actually doing something else on the other end of the phone. She can see her drifting about their apartment with the phone on that long cord, trailing after the maid and fussing, stopping by a mirror to check her hair is what it should be, wondering whether she's got time to meet a girl-friend before her husband gets home.

Margot puts the receiver down, but it doesn't take long for her excitement to return, and she hangs out with Sarah and Evangeline, who pretend to be thrilled too, and mostly are, though each of them would have killed to be made Queen themselves. Still, if they can't be Queen, being the best friends of the Queen gives them some kind of reflected glory, and they roll along with Margot for the rest of the day, stopping to bask in each conversation for as long as they can.

Have you heard?

Oh yes, isn't it wonderful?

She's going to look so stunning.

So it goes, until it's time for lights out, and then, as Margot closes her eyes, she knows she's done the wrong thing.

Immediately, Isobel is there, her eyes staring unblinking, the unblinking, unflinching gaze of the dead, the dead who can look at anything and not be scared; the dead who can face any horror and not look away; the dead, who see nothing, but on whose face everything horrific can be seen.

Isobel floats above her, but she is not wet this time.

Margot struggles and cries but no sound comes from her mouth. Without warning, Isobel drops onto her, and they become one writhing body, spinning and twisting in Margot's sheets. Margot thrashes to be free, but Isobel is too strong, and they twist themselves tighter and tighter in the white sheets, like a rope twisting up and up.

Evangeline runs down the hall to Mrs Grenjard's room, and the days to Procession Day tick away, pages of a calendar slowly curling up like withering leaves, falling to the ground.

10

The pilgrim of the labyrinth

Jack Lewis sits in his room. He ought to go for breakfast: there's a long day ahead of him, his busiest of the week. But he's thinking about Isobel again. It must have been some time after he'd loaned her those books that they met by chance again, in town. It was a Sunday, when the girls were allowed a little liberty and leeway. Mostly they would flock to town in groups of three or four, usually to drink soda on the terrace of the Red Lion until that fat and pompous ass who thought he was in charge told them to clear out.

Jack had been taking his usual Sunday stroll when he'd met Isobel a little way out of town, where Church Street meets Main. She was about to walk past without making eye contact. Jack wanted her to stop. He'd loaned her some books, he'd tried to reach out to her. He thought she would at least stop and thank him, or say something.

Rather than asking about the books, he made a connection to the cemetery.

'You ever been in there?' he'd asked, and Isobel had stopped then.

She gave a tiny shake of her head. She looked desolate. Empty, and it hurt Jack too much.

'You might like it,' he said, forcing as much brightness into his voice as a miserable fifty-four-year-old could possibly manage.

Again, nothing.

'You like spirals, right?'

She'd nodded.

Jack held up a hand, smiling.

'Come with me.'

He'd led the way into the cemetery, past the orderly rows of graves; the patches of Civil War dead, the imposing tombs of local dignitaries, the crumbling stones of the earliest settlers in Stockbridge.

She'd walked slowly beside him, and he could almost hear the pain inside her. *How hard it is to be young*, he thought. But, *How hard it is to get old* came straight after that.

In the farthest corner of the cemetery stood a somewhat forgotten corner, surrounded by a circle of tall yews. A gap between two of the trees made room for a narrow path to enter a circle of graves; in fact, a series of circles of graves.

Then, Isobel understood, and her surprise was enough to bring words to her lips, without agonising thought beforehand.

'It's a spiral . . .' she'd whispered, and wandered dream-like between the stones.

Jack nodded.

'It looks like circles at first, doesn't it? A series of concentric circles. But you're right, it's one big spiral.'

She'd turned, her eyes brighter than he'd seen them before.

'Who . . . ?'

'Who made it?'

'This is the Siegelton Spiral. Begun by an

ancestor of our school's founder, Ida. That's her grave, right there. And in the centre is the great-grand-daddy of them all, Judge Theodore Siegelton.'

He nodded towards the centre of the spiral. From where they stood at the outer arms of the spiral, the graves wound in and in towards the inevitable centre; where a large monument, a four-sided obelisk, struck up into the air.

Isobel was already heading towards it, but Jack smiled to see that, rather than walk straight to it, cutting across the winding arm of the spiral, Isobel was following it round and round, taking the long path, twisting slowly towards the centre.

'Like a pilgrim of old,' he'd called out.

'Sir?'

'Nothing,' he'd replied. 'Go on with your journey, pilgrim. Go and look.'

He watched her wind her way in.

Jack Lewis remembered something.

In the old churches, the cathedrals of Europe, winding labyrinths were laid in patterns of stone. Pilgrims would crawl on hands and knees around the paths, making their way to the centre. He'd seen one such maze in Chartres, when he was with the Fifth Armoured Division in France, in '44. Suspected of harbouring German lookouts, their orders were to bomb the cathedral into the ground, but his CO, Colonel Griffith, had questioned the decision. He'd volunteered to scout behind enemy lines to find out if it was really necessary to destroy this unbelievable achievement of man's noblest creativity, and proved that the cathedral was unoccupied. The cathedral was saved. Colonel Griffith had taken one enlisted man with him; a youngish Jack Lewis, who had stared at the maze on the floor of the nave.

His CO had come up behind him.

'It's not a maze, Private. It's a labyrinth.'

'Sir?'

'It's a labyrinth. A maze has false turnings, dead ends, tricks to trap you forever. A labyrinth, on the other hand, is just one path, wound up around itself. All it takes to reach the centre is for you to show devotion. All it asks of you is perseverance. All it asks of you is that you dedicate yourself to it. Show faith, pilgrim, and you will make it to the end.'

Colonel Griffith had patted Jack on the shoulder, and walked away, leaving him to stare open-mouthed at the retreating back of his CO, who had never uttered a single word before that wasn't about warfare.

Jack had taken one last look at the labyrinth, and then turned and scurried after his CO, realising as he did so that Colonel Griffith hadn't just been talking about patterns on the floors of churches, but that he'd been talking about life, and death. And so he had been talking about the war, after all.

Show faith, pilgrim, and you will make it to the end.

He'd always remembered that, or almost always. Sometimes these things get lost under layers of dead leaves.

Colonel Griffith, however, had not made it to the end. Later that afternoon, as they'd headed north out of the city, he'd led an attack on a position of some fifteen enemy soldiers, and had been killed by machine-gun fire.

Standing in the Stockbridge cemetery that afternoon, watching Isobel wind her way to the centre, Colonel Griffith's words came back to him from across the years. He'd thought about them many times, but it was only then as he watched the fragile girl making her way that he realised that, though the labyrinth can take many forms, its simplest expression is the spiral.

The spiral is the simplest of labyrinths, and all it asks is that you show it devotion. Then you will make it to the end.

Jack sits, as breakfast comes and goes without him, and remembers Isobel, the pilgrim.

11

Such a little thing

Eveline Grenjard is less delighted with the choice of Margot as Procession Queen. She is only mildly insulted that for the first time in years Miss Grant has not consulted her for her opinion. That's not what upsets her. What upsets her is that Margot is exactly the kind of girl that she despises.

She stops herself.

Walking around inside Eveline's mind is a pleasant thing; for we find that she is not the kind of person to despise anyone, not really. She is a kind woman who does the best she can by all her girls. It's just that some of them require more understanding, more patience than others and Margot is one of those girls who pushes her tolerance to the limit.

Yes, Eveline knows that Margot's parents are that typical cliché of the unloving rich, with their place on Central Park West and a summerhouse in the Hamptons. She's seen precious little of Margot's parents during her time at Foxgrove, but she's seen enough. So she understands why Margot is the way she is; shallow, spiteful, vain. But that doesn't make it much easier to bear.

So as she patrols Siegelton House one night after lights out, and finds Margot not only awake and chatting to Evangeline, but chewing gum in bed, she hits the roof.

She marches over to Margot and holds out her hand, covering it with a handkerchief.

'Spit it out,' she snaps, and Margot slowly, reluctantly, pops the gum out.

She rolls her eyes at Evangeline, but then Mrs Grenjard starts to rummage through Margot's stuff, pulling out desk drawers, rifling through her clothes, with angry haste.

'Hey!' Margot shouts. 'You can't do that! Stop it. Hey, you *cannot* do that. When my parents –'

Mrs Grenjard shoots her such a withering look at the mention of her parents that it's enough to silence Margot for a moment. But then she sees that Mrs Grenjard has her bag in her hands and is shaking it upside down over the bed.

Among other forbidden items; lipstick, a condom. Then four packs of gum fall out. Four.

Mrs Grenjard snatches them up and adds them to the gum in her handkerchief.

'What the hell are you doing?' shouts Margot.

Evangeline is horrified.

'Margot! Margot, don't. Don't make it worse.'

Speechlessly, Mrs Grenjard marches away down the corridor, and Margot scrambles after her.

'Margot! Don't!'

The whole floor is awake by now, and a few heads emerge from doors in time to see Mrs Grenjard fling the bathroom door open, and head straight to the toilet bowl. As Margot flounders in the doorway of the bathroom, she's in time to see Mrs Grenjard holding her stuff over the bowl.

'Don't you dare!' screams Margot, and then Mrs Grenjard opens her hand, letting everything fall into the pan, flushing as soon as it hits the water.

'You bitch! You absolute bitch!' screams Margot, though Evangeline is there now, pulling her away, trying to get her to come back to bed.

Mrs Grenjard doesn't say another word, but marches back to her own room, leaving Evangeline to wrestle a still furious Margot back to bed.

'Margot, leave it. You'll be in such trouble! Leave it. It's only a few packs of gum, for God's sake.'

At that, Margot whirls round at her.

'What the hell would you know about it?'

She shoves her away, And Evangeline falls back onto her bed, staring at Margot, wide-eyed with horror and rejection combined.

12

Three days of
summer sun

Nathaniel Drake thinks about his future.
He sits alone in the staff room one sunny
lunchtime, smoking a cigarette. He made
that trip to Boston, where some old miser in
an antiquarian bookstore offered him fifteen
hundred dollars for the Sarafian first edition.
He knows it's worth double that, and the
suspicion that the book dealer was trying to
cheat him has left him sore.

*Thinks I'm an idiot. I'll take it to New York
next time I'm home. Get a proper price for it.*

Life at Foxgrove has soured very quickly.
He is no longer sure he wants to be there.
He doesn't belong and he no longer feels like
he owns the place.

Miss Ellery, the Art teacher, comes into the room.

'Bum one of those?' she says, pointing at his cigarette.

Get your own, he thinks.

'Sure,' he says, pulling out his packet and proffering it to her. Frances Ellery isn't so bad, he tells himself. Good legs. Shame about that nose.

She sighs heavily as she drags on the cigarette.

'Bad day?' he says. 'I know how you feel. This is a strange place.'

'Oh, don't mind me,' she answers. 'I always feel the pace by this point of the year. Need the summer break. Oh, I know there are only three days to go and one of those is Procession Day, but I could die right now.'

'What's with this Procession Day, anyway? Seems kind of weird to me.'

'Old school tradition,' says Miss Ellery. 'Goes all the way back to the start, apparently. I quite like it. It shortens the term by a day and that's fine by me. I'm dreading this one, though.'

'Yeah?'

'Well, yes. After . . . You weren't here, of course. But you know, it was all cancelled last year. So this one is going to be quite a tense affair. Weeping girls, no doubt. Oh, I know I sound mean. I'm not. I just want a nice quiet day so we can all get out of here for the summer.'

'So that girl,' says Drake. 'Isobel, right?'

'You heard of her? Yes, Isobel. What about her?'

'So, does anyone know why she did it?'

Miss Ellery shrugs.

'Who knows? Who knows what goes through the mind of someone who . . .'

She trails off.

'Yeah, but what a way to go. Drowning yourself.'

Miss Ellery looks up sharply.

'Is that what you heard? She drowned herself? No, she didn't drown herself. She . . .' Miss Ellery holds her breath for a moment. Then blurts out, 'Oh, it's too awful.'

And with that, the apparently cool Miss Ellery gets up from her chair, and runs to the bathroom in floods of tears.

13

The rain hides everything

Daniel Larsen knows everyone in Stockbridge, or everyone with a car, and that's pretty much the same thing. He likes his work well enough. His father, 'Man' Larsen, makes him work too hard, but then he makes himself work too hard as well. It's their way, Man tells his son, often.

We work hard in this family, son. We work hard. So one day we won't have to.

That day never seems to come.

Daniel is seventeen, but working at the gas station and around the body shop has made him strong for his age. He doesn't go to school any more, something that he didn't much care for anyway, glad as he was to get away from the likes of Jimmy Harkness. His parents own the store and a couple of other businesses in town and have made some money, which they seem to spend on their only son all too freely, an almost new Dodge Dart for his birthday being the most notable example.

Of course, there's nowhere else in town to get gas, but even if there were, Daniel reckons that Jimmy would still swing by their station once a week just to make him fill it up while he leans against the white of the hood, smirking.

Today is such a day.

Daniel stares at nothing, his eyes fixing on the car. There's a small dent on the roof of Jimmy's Dart and he starts to imagine fixing it, as he has fixed so many minor dings in people's cars. He focuses on the dent.

When he's done pumping, and Jimmy has paid his dollars and swung out of the forecourt, Daniel sighs and drops his shoulders. For some reason, whenever Jimmy comes by, he feels like there will be a fight. Perhaps there will be, one day. But not today.

Daniel lifts his head and sees something

he cannot avoid seeing, but which will, very soon, be enough to tell his old man that he's leaving. For good. Starting over, somewhere new. Somewhere without the memories.

What Daniel sees is some Foxgrove girls, walking along Main Street, in their uniform, and that uniform starts him thinking, remembering things he would rather not remember, as it always does.

He wasn't allowed to keep her letter.

It was evidence, they said. For some reason, he would have liked to have kept it, but he wasn't allowed to. It was evidence, though he's not sure what it was evidence of. Instead, they left him with the memories.

It was raining that night.

In his mind, it's raining now, as he remembers it all, again.

It's raining.

It had been clear when he left home, but the rain comes on as he makes his way through the woods.

He makes his way out of town, onto

Siegelton land, and to the bridge, just after nine. He hadn't been able to get away sooner, because his mother and father had gone to a church meeting and left him to tidy up and put the twins to bed. He'd thought twice about leaving the twins at all, but they were eight, and he'd been pumping gas when he was eight, something his father seems to have forgotten.

He hasn't brought a torch. It had been clear enough to see without one before the rain, but as it got heavier, almost all light has been lost. Still, he knows the way. He used to go trespassing here with other kids when he was little; he's been to the bridge a hundred times, could do it with his eyes shut.

Still, the rain is getting heavier and that slows him some more. He liked what she'd said in her letter. Even if he didn't feel the same way, it was nice to read things like that. He owed her something, he figured. He owed her something at least.

Then, he does get lost. In woods he knows so well, he's lost, and in the end, it's only because he sees the lights from the school in the distance that he picks up his bearings again. In the driving rain, it's hard to be sure, but he thinks he hears something. A voice. Crying out.

Then, he can see the shape of the bridge, a darker shape emerging from the darkness all around. He knows he'll be dry in there.

There was that part in her letter he didn't like so well, of course. He wondered what she meant by it; it sounded bad to him, but he supposes she's a girl with an imagination, like some he went to school with, though never much spoke to.

It's pitch black as he makes his way onto the bridge and under the cover of the roof. He pauses for a moment, grateful to be able to wipe the water from his eyes, straining to see, but he can see nothing.

Maybe she's gone. She said nine. Maybe she didn't wait. Maybe she got scared.

Then he thinks, *God, maybe she wasn't kidding. That bad part in the letter . . .*

He runs forward in the dark, trips and

finds himself under the broken section of roof, where the rain pours on him once more.

He stands, and there's a broken section in the lattice of the wall. He feels for it in the dark, and leans out, looking down at the pool where they used to dive as kids, though they knew it was dangerous. They knew all the stories, and yet they jumped in anyway, but on bright hot days, with all their friends whooping and cheering, not in the middle of rain-pounded nights like this, in the cold, and the dark.

Staring down at the water, he can see nothing, only hear its roar and the drumming of the rain on the roof of the bridge.

He calls out her name.

'Isobel!'

It feels strange to say her name aloud. They've never even spoken.

'Isobel! It's me, Daniel. Daniel Larsen. Are you there?'

He backs away from the wall.

Tap.

He stops moving.

He stops moving, at the very first tap.

Tap, tap.

A coldness surges into him, because something is very wrong and he knows it.

Tap, tap, on his shoulder, just a gentle tap on his shoulder blade, and then another.

He holds his breath, and then ducks away, spinning round.

'Who's there?' he shouts, trying to sound angry, though all he is is terrified.

Nothing.

Nothing comes to him through the vibrating dark air.

Something drags across his vision. An even deeper darkness than that of the bridge.

It could be yards away. It could be right before his face.

He reaches out, up, with a shaking hand, slowly, and his fingers meet something right in front of his face.

Tap.

His fingers close around the thing, and though his fingers feel a familiar shape, his mind cannot work out what he is touching at first. And then it comes to him.

Toes.

He is holding toes, a foot. In the air.

He shudders and falls back, a wordless yell dying in his throat.

He sits in the mud, panting with fear, his blood thumping, and then, he thinks something important.

Maybe she's not dead.

He scrambles up onto the lattice of the wall, reaches, and there she is, hanging from a rafter in the dark. His fingers reach out into the air and he finds her face, her neck. They are both warm.

There is a rope at her neck. She sways as he touches her.

He tries to reach for the rope, to find a way to loosen it, to free her.

'Isobel!' he yells. 'Isobel! Don't be dead. Don't!'

But she is and in the end it's another half an hour before he makes it home, and out again with his father and the sheriff not far behind, when they finally cut her down and lay her in the mud of the bridge, still, and cold, and wet.

14

Procession Day

Miss Grant leads the lines of teachers and girls out onto the lawn.

It is a fierce, sunlit day. Warm since the first. Warm and still, without a wavering breath of breeze to disturb the leaves on the sycamores that surround Ida Siegelton's precious lawn. There were twelve girls that first year, that first Procession. Today there are over two hundred, all of whom will make a spiral, but only twenty-six of whom will form the final spiral of the day, the Seniors, led by a girl chosen from across the school to symbolise their equality.

Today, however, it will be a Senior who leads the final dance as Procession Queen; Margot.

She steps into the sunlight, dressed only in white, as are all the girls; bedecked in long white dresses that stroke the grass.

The parents watch from rows of seats placed on three of the four sides of the lawn, and crane their heads and nudge and point and smile and weep as their little girls step out, so serious and proud.

The rows of girls are forming on the fourth side of the square, waiting for the first spiral to begin. Their teachers are spaced among them, and the other staff. Jack Lewis has seen enough of these dances to last a lifetime, for Nathaniel Drake, it is all new, and yet his mind is elsewhere. Yesterday he made the trip back to Boston and settled for the fifteen hundred.

Miser, he thinks, and he keeps thinking that way until Margot appears. Since she is the Queen, who will lead, she arrives last, in pride of her place. Then Drake's eyes are on her. Jack Lewis watches him watching her, and then his gaze drifts to Eveline Grenjard. The Siegelton Housemother stands at one end, next to the line of processing girls, and she cannot help but look at Margot as she walks by.

Margot has been full of herself all week. Only yesterday she made a big fuss about asking whether she'd had any mail, and when Mrs Grenjard had handed over a small packet postmarked NYC, Margot had given her a smile the meaning of which was hard to find.

Now, however, the meaning of the smile is all too obvious. For as Margot passes Eveline Grenjard, she turns her head slowly, making sure they have full eye contact, and then opens her mouth just enough to deliberately display the gum she's chewing.

It's all Mrs Grenjard can do to prevent herself stepping out of line and slapping Margot's face. She even visualises herself doing it, and sees the gum flying from her mouth and falling in some little girl's hair.

The girls have finished lining up, Miss Grant makes a short speech, the parents applaud, and the first dance begins.

From time to time Eveline glances over

at Margot, who is slowly and ostentatiously chewing.

To Mrs Grenjard, Margot is a disgrace. To Nathaniel, she looks incredible. She has chosen a dress that borders on the risqué, with a very low-cut neckline and a skirt through which her legs are clearly visible when the sun shines in just the right way. Mrs Grenjard puts her head down and hopes to God that Miss Grant is too busy with her little speeches to notice anything, but then, as the afternoon wears on, and the final dance approaches, the spiral begins to unravel.

The first thing: Margot misses her cue to lead the line for the grand final dance. Jennifer nudges her and still she doesn't move. Her eyes seem to be fixed on the trees at the edge of the woodland. Jennifer nudges her again and hisses in her ear.

A parent coughs nervously – not Margot's own parents, who sit stony-faced as their daughter bungles her big moment. But then she's on the move, though she seems not to really be there. She heads off towards the wrong end of the lawn, and Jennifer pulls her elbow to put her straight. For a moment or two, everything is fine; Margot leading the line, holding the school flag, and the other Seniors follow, to a round of rapturous applause from the crowd.

She starts to spiral in, and then, as the loop first closes on itself, she stops dead. Jennifer, who'd been smiling at her parents, walks into the back of her, and a loud mutter ripples through the parents. Jennifer shoves Margot.

'For God's sake!' she hisses. 'What are you doing?'

But Margot doesn't hear.

The voices of ghosts come out of the air. She cannot understand them, but she doesn't need to understand the words in order to feel their meaning. The spiral world unfurls and Margot's mind breaks.

She drops the flag, and begins to back away. Her eyes are fixed towards the woodland, where she seems to see something that no one else sees.

She takes another step back, trips over the

hem of her long white dress, and falls to the grass.

Teachers rush forwards.

It's a hot day. The excitement. She's fainted.

But no, Margot has not fainted, her eyes roll in her head and yet still she can see what no one else can see; Isobel Milewski, walking steadily across the lawn towards her, dressed in white winding sheets, a noose of rope hanging from her hand.

Margot screams, and the gum falls from her mouth and into the soft grass, where it lies, forgotten. That gum, which arrived yesterday in a small parcel from NYC, sent by that willing if somewhat spliffed-out friend of Margot's grown-up cousin Tom. That gum, which always arrives in packets that have been opened and carefully re-sealed. That gum, in which the sticks are stuck together in twos. And the day before yesterday, when Tom's spliffed-out friend was making the packs up, did someone talk to him just as he was hovering over two of the sticks, eye-dropper in hand? They did. Someone spoke to him, and then, well, he wasn't sure whether he'd put a couple of drops on that stick of gum, so he shrugged, and put on a couple more. Then he smirked and put on a couple more still, just for kicks, placed the covering stick on top, and sent it all off to that prim little witch at her fancy private school. What did he care? Money's money, and she always paid over the odds without blinking.

Margot writhes backwards in the grass, and all thoughts of the Procession Day being a proud recovery after last year's no-show are lost. People crowd around, too many people, trying to calm her, but it's not working. All she can see is Isobel, still walking through the crowd, and then, to Margot's horror, every face around her changes into Isobel's face, peering at her and leaning in, though she can still tell the real Isobel, for she's the one with a noose on her hand.

The noose starts to move, and she sees that it's not made of rope, but it's a snake, a coiling snake, from whose fangs drips acid.

The younger girls watch in horror and dismay, some of the older ones are crying, their parents hurrying them away, while yet others stand with arms folded.

Joan turns to her friend Natalie.

'Told you.'

Natalie nods, open-mouthed.

'I thought you were kidding.'

Joan shakes her head.

'Bad trip.'

Margot's mind is beyond reach now.

Inside, it is a turmoil, a maelstrom of memory and fear and hallucination. Lost somewhere in there is the memory of writing letters, two of them.

She showed them to Evangeline and Sarah, who giggled and nodded, though Sarah had asked, 'Why the different times?'

'Let's make her wait a bit. See what she does.'

Two letters.

One from Isobel to Daniel.

One from Daniel to Isobel.

The one from Isobel to Daniel, declaring her love and begging for a meeting at the covered bridge, ended up in the court files after the inquest. And the other? It waits, still to be found.

Evangeline had doubted it would work. Margot had herself, in some ways, which was why she'd made a date with Jimmy to drive down to the bridge a little later to have some fun.

But it did work.

Isobel had arrived at eight thirty, as the letter from Daniel had told her to. Margot and the others watched from across the water, hidden in the bushes, and it was all they could do not to giggle so loud as to give the game away.

The minutes had ticked by, crawling towards nine, and all Isobel had done was stare into the water. And it was drizzling.

'This is boring,' whispered Sarah, and Margot was angry. She hissed at Sarah, but it was true. They should have made the times the same in each letter, and she was just about to tell Sarah it was her fault, when they saw the lights on Jimmy's Dodge crawling over the old leaf-strewn road.

'Idiot,' Margot hissed, as the rain started to

fall heavily. 'He's early. I told him half after. Come on, we're getting wet. Let's go down and have some fun.'

It was nine o'clock. Daniel should have been there. He would have been there, but for the twins, and the dark, and the rain.

Then, there they were.

Jimmy, and his dumb friend Jack, come along for the ride and the chance to meet some girls.

Margot, Sarah and Evangeline.

And between them, caught in the lights of the Dodge, Isobel.

'Didn't your lover show up?' Margot teased, and they all laughed. 'What was it that you expected to find?'

Isobel tried to push past them, but they grab her.

'Not leaving so soon, are you?'

'What about this nice young man?' Margot said, pointing at the grinning Jack. 'Why don't you have him, instead?'

Jack sniggered and Jimmy thumped him on the shoulder.

'Leave me alone,' was all Isobel said, and even that was too much.

Thinks she's too good for you.

Stuck-up bitch.

No one's going to love you, you freak.

It was one minute after nine.

In the next minute, the game escalated into something more sinister.

You may as well end it now.

Or spend your life on your own.

Freak.

Isobel made another attempt to run, but they had her.

Jump! Jump! Jump!

No! Wait! Maybe she can swim real good. She needs to make sure.

That was Jimmy's idea. He had a length of tow rope in the truck of the Dodge, and it didn't take long to throw it over a rafter in the roof of the bridge.

Jack and Margot pushed Isobel onto the roof of the car, and then Sarah and Evangeline followed and they made her stand up straight while they put the noose over her head, screaming with delight as they did, hollering and shouting at Isobel, who cried and begged for them to stop.

And they *were* only playing around. They all knew that, as they climbed off the roof of the car, and left Isobel standing on her own, rope round her neck so tight that, though she tried to free herself, the noose wouldn't loosen.

They were only playing around, as Margot grinned at Jimmy.

Give her a scare.

And he was only playing around as he edged the car forward with a sudden jolt, so that Isobel had to dance quick to stay on her feet, and they all laughed, and they were laughing still as he did it again, and then as he did it a third time, his foot slipped from the rainwater on the sole of his sneakers, and the car shot forward, almost hitting Margot and Sarah.

They screamed, and then they screamed again.

Isobel's feet dangled in the red tail-lights and her body jerked.

Sarah screamed.

Margot yelled at Jimmy.

Get the car back! Get it back!

Jack was trying to hold her legs, to hold her up, but it was not enough to take her weight.

Get the car back!

But Jimmy had stalled the Dodge and it would not start. He tried again and again, screaming nothing as he did.

Jack tried to hold Isobel.

Help me! Help me!

But Sarah lay on the ground screaming, and Evangeline just stood and stared.

The car started.

Isobel's body had stopped moving.

It was three minutes after nine.

The five looked at each other, then Margot climbed into the car, dragging the girls after her, and Jack.

Drive.

So they drove.

At six minutes after nine o'clock, Daniel Larsen arrived to meet the girl he'd never met, but who said she loved him. That was what she'd said in her letter.

And the other letter, that 'Daniel' had written to 'Isobel'?

The letter in which he declared love for this quiet and harmless girl, whose true beauty was on the inside of her.

That small note still waits to be found, tucked away, unseen by all, inside the final few pages of a first edition of the book of poetry by James Sarafian known as *Stockbridge, and Other Poems*, and sits in the window of an antiquarian book dealer in Boston.

Stockbridge

There, when earth was cooling,
and air was young.
The gate. The apple tree.
The wet grass.
Sunshine. Geese.
Water.
The face of the Divine.

At Foxes Grove, the maidens dance a volta.
Their winding steps describe the path
of an eternity of leavings.
For every girl that goes,
another joins the renewed and infinite line:
Sorcery
winding from the earth

drawn up and around.
So, they dance in lambent light,
across the dew-wet grass
till torchlight lures them from the lawn
and lays them in their beds
where it seems their legs still turn
as they spiral down to sleep.

I renounce belief.

Why have you come?
says a voice from the air,
and what was it that you expected to find?
You who have come to trouble the dead.
You whose voice was swallowed by dark
should know the path that was laid for you.
Through the gate, under the apple tree,
across the wet grass.

I renounce belief in going home.

And those who never smiled at the sun,
and lay on thorns, watching the moon,
the thirsty, the hungering, the hollow,

the trodden-down.
Those who watched the damaged stars,
waiting for One who would never come
while beyond the final, broken gate
the voices of ghosts come out of the air.
What was it that you expected to find?

And what *did* you expect?
Satisfaction, understanding?
Salvation before the ending of the days?
Yet, just around the turn of the stair,
a glimmer of torchlight awaits your
    discovery.

I renounce belief.
I renounce belief in going home.
And with that thought
the chemical action of radiant energy
strips us of delusions,
destroys those thoughts that would hold us
    back,
would have us turn back, forever.

Thus, illuminated, we are free,

and turning to your friend you say:
It is enough to know that not to know is
    enough.
It is enough not to know.

And what you could not hope for, you found.
Wet grass under your hands and knees,
sunlight falling through the apple tree,
and protection.
And then, in the stillness
between breaths;
redemption, safety, and love.

Did you enjoy *Killing the Dead*?
Don't miss Marcus Sedgwick's other novels.

—

The GHOSTS of HEAVEN

—

MIDWINTERBLOOD

—

SHE IS NOT INVISIBLE

—

BLOOD RED, SNOW WHITE

—

The BOOK of DEAD DAYS

—

The DARK FLIGHT DOWN

—

The DARK HORSE

—

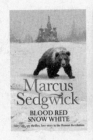
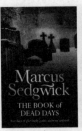
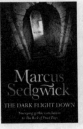
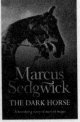

FLOODLAND

—

The FORESHADOWING

—

MY SWORDHAND is SINGING

—

The KISS of DEATH

—

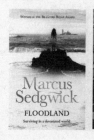

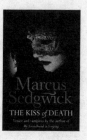

REVOLVER

—

WHITE CROW

—

WITCH HILL

—

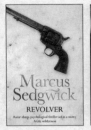
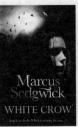

You might also enjoy reading Alan Gibbons. Here is an extract from his latest novel

HATE

Teenage Kicks

Saturday, 10 August 2013

The last time I saw Rosie, she was getting on the bus with Paul. It was August and the air was thick with dust and petrol fumes on the Manchester road. Off to our left, on the far side of the housing estate, sun and shadow were playing tag on the hills. Some of the people at the stop noticed the young couple next to them. Rosie and Paul didn't seem to notice. They were used to the attention. I found myself smiling. Rosie never minded. Jewels glitter. It is in their nature. That's what they do. They shine while other people, like me, live their lives unseen.

Then Rosie did something out of character. She called to me across the road as I walked away. She was beautiful, so tiny and perfect, but she made her statement by the way she dressed. She was quiet;, happy in the skin she had made for herself. So when she called my name it was unexpected.

'Eve,' she cried. '*Teenage Kicks*.'

Mum had been playing it just before we left. She had looked up from her assignment. She used YouTube as a distraction when she needed a break. It was the way our family was, I suppose. We communicated through music, recommended the songs we listened to and enjoyed together.

'Do you want to hear perfection?'

I remember Rosie wrinkling her nose, teasing. She loved it really. She adored music, any kind of music, not just the doomy stuff I heard coming through the wall, but Sugababes, Abba, anything at all. The Undertones played to the end, then I said I would walk with her to the stop. Paul strode along beside us while we talked.

'Eve. *Teenage Kicks.*'

And she started to dance, her long, black skirt swaying, her slender arms and small hands weaving patterns. It was as if she was drawing a portrait of her soul in the air. I danced too, copying her every move. The memory of the music played in my head and we laughed with each new twist and turn. Her hair swung and the hot sun was bright on her face. That's how I remember her, laughing and glowing in the bright play of the light. Then Paul tapped her on the shoulder and the bus came between us. I watched them settling into their seats and waved. One last time Rosie's arms fluttered. One last time I copied her. Then she was gone.

Gone forever.

Monday, 24 February 2014

I had that image of Rosie in my head when Jess's elbow jabbed my ribs, calling me back to Monday registration, the scraped chairs, the fitful yawns, the general air of boredom. In the corridor, a door slammed.

'Hey, look what the wind blew in.'

The newcomer had collar-length, blond hair and fine features. He was tall, lean and athletic-looking, but there was an awkwardness about him that diminished him somehow, and made him seem smaller than he was. I watched him with growing curiosity. He was backing against the wall, as if trying to melt into it. I recognised something of myself in the guarded way he sidled into the classroom. Some people announce themselves to the world. Others dip beneath its scrutiny. I waited for Mrs Rawmarsh to introduce him. When she said his name my heart slammed.

'This is Anthony Broad.'

She pronounced it Anthony with the accent on the 'th' as in thump. I glimpsed Jess's lips repeating the three syllables silently. She could be so predictable. She's great, but the moment she falls for some boy it's as if she becomes him, adopting his rhythms of speech, his attitudes, his ideas, no matter how stupid they sound.

Only when the first rush of attraction is over does she become herself again. I love her for her loyalty and fun, but sometimes the wild enthusiasms drive me crazy.

'You don't fancy him?'

We'd been here a few times now. Jess likes boys and they like her. She gets their attention with the way she walks, the way she talks, the intent way she listens, the infectious way she laughs. She makes everyone in her company feel special.

'What's not to fancy? He's fit. Oh, come on, Eve, lighten up.'

I had a different reason to dwell on his name. It walked into my mind and stood in a darkened corner like an uninvited guest at a wedding. That name . . . Broad. Anthony Broad.

Registration over, we shouldered our bags and stepped into the corridor. I felt the press of Jess's fingers on my forearm.

'Eve, pretend to say something to me. He's coming over.'

Why all the excitement? I refused to play Jess's games and stayed completely silent.

'Hi Anthony.'

She was like one of those little terriers that rolls on its back and invites you to tickle its tummy. She was happy and bright-eyed, sending out signals without an iota of self-consciousness. What if it really was him? I rummaged in my bag for some imaginary object so I didn't have to make eye contact. I left that to Jess. She had all the eye contact of a peacock's tail. She was so, so eager to impress, and I was drowning.

Broad.

Anthony Broad.

'Do you think you could help me?' he mumbled. 'Everything is kind of confusing. How do I get to L29?'

'L is for Languages,' Jess explained. 'All the Arts and Humanities are down there. It goes English, Geography, History, Languages. It's alphabetical. Pastoral Care and RE are off to the right. Maths and Science are down the other end of the school. Zoology's at the end.'

'There's a Zoology department?'

'No. That was a joke.'

'Oh.'

Jess looked perturbed.

'Obviously not a very good joke,' she said.

Her wide eyes and pouting lips didn't seem to be working their usual magic. Anthony's mind was elsewhere. He didn't seem to have listened to a word she'd said.

'Oh, right.'

The second word dropped away, apologetic. His uncertain gaze followed the way she was pointing.

'I see.'

Jess giggled. She was dog whistle high and invitingly cute. Some boys like that. This best friend didn't.

'You don't get it at all, do you?'

I glanced his way and saw his uncertainty evolve into a thin smile.

'Not really.'

The crowds hurrying between classes buffeted us. Girls dissolved into laughter, boys leapt on their mates' backs, teachers weaved wearily through the tumult, casting the odd, disapproving eye. Everybody had a purpose but, at the centre of the crush, Anthony didn't. For that moment he was the eye of the storm.

'Come with us. We're going to L29 too. Spanish, yeah?'

'Right. Spanish.'

I was willing Jess to stop. Why did she have to adopt him as if he was a stray dog? Surely he could find L29 by himself? Kids start new schools all the time. Why did she have to roll out the red carpet for this one? He could see where we were going. All he had to do was follow us. But Jess just chattered away.

'How come you moved school? People usually stay put in Year 11, GCSEs and all that.'

Anthony looked uncomfortable. I could see the thoughts turning over in his mind. His face betrayed him as he considered first one answer then another. Jess came at it another way.

'Where was your last school?'

'Brierley.'

I heard the way he said it, as a kind of confession. Brierley. That's where it happened. In Cartmel Park. Oh God, my first instincts were right.

'Why did you move?'

There was that same moment of discomfort.

'Family stuff. You know.'

We reached L29. Anthony made a beeline for the back row and sat in the corner, by the window, staring out across the moors. I knew that distant look. I knew that aching detachment. But he was no kindred spirit. He was my opposite. Anthony Broad. It was him. It had to be. Jess frowned a question. What was I thinking? I smiled and shrugged. That seemed to reassure her.

Miss Munoz swept into the room, stopped, briefly registering Anthony's presence then fumbled for the small, grey remote to start the whiteboard projector. It purred into life. The failing bulb cast a gloomy light on the screen. Dust motes swirled. Miss Munoz started the lesson the way she always did, with the date and the weather. Then she asked us all what we did over the weekend. Some made an effort. Some grunted. Others grinned and said something stupid to wind her up. Most of us just fidgeted and hoped she would pass us by.

It was Monday, 24 February, less than six months after that night, after what happened to Rosie.